JA

Everyday Ghosts

A Fable

James Morrison is the author of a memoir, *Broken Fever*, and a novel, *The Lost Girl,* among other books. His collection of short stories, *Said and Done*, was a finalist for a Lambda Literary Award and winner of a *ForeWord* Book of the Year award. James Morrison teaches at Claremont McKenna College.

GEMMA
Open Door

First published by GemmaMedia in 2011.

GemmaMedia
230 Commercial Street
Boston, MA 02109 USA

www.gemmamedia.com

Printed in the United States of America

15 14 13 12 11 1 2 3 4 5

978-1-934848-82-1

Library of Congress Cataloging-in-Publication Data
Morrison, James, 1960–
Everyday ghosts : a fable / James Morrison.
p. cm. — (Gemma open door)
ISBN 978-1-934848-82-1 (pbk.)
1. Monks—Fiction. 2. Self-realization—Fiction. 3. Psychological fiction. I. Title.
PS3563.O87458E94 2011
813'.54—dc22
2011017558

Cover by Night & Day Design

Inspired by the Irish series of books designed for adult literacy, Gemma Open Door Foundation provides fresh stories, new ideas, and essential resources for young people and adults as they embrace the power of reading and the written word.

Brian Bouldrey
North American Series Editor

GEMMA
Open Door

For Joseph Marchione

1

Pete heard it before he saw it, the quick whoosh of the stick through the air, and the thwack-thwack-thwack as it hit Neb's backside. In the clearing, Louis raised the stick over his head to strike again, but Pete was too fast and snatched it away. Louis stood with his mouth gaping and his arm stretched out. Pete wanted to give his open palm a clean smack, but he snapped the stick in two and dropped it to the ground. Neb let out a snuffle and dug a hoof into the dirt, kicking up dust.

"If I ever catch you doing that again," Pete began, but he knew as soon as he said them that his words were not well chosen, so he stopped. He took Neb's rope and led her up the hill.

"Brother Louis told me what happened," said Father Gabriel when he called Pete in the next morning. "I know there are two sides to every story."

There were more than that, but when Pete spoke to Father Gabriel, their talks did split in two, what Pete answered and what was left unspoken. "He beat Neb again," said Pete.

"The mule was not hauling," said Father Gabriel. "Brother Louis nudged it to encourage its cooperation."

"Neb's a donkey," said Pete. "He beat her with a stick."

Father Gabriel put his hands together, touching at the fingertips, and took a breath. "Let man have power over the fish of the sea, the birds of the air, and the cattle. That is Genesis. You may have come across it in your reading. Notice that the cattle are singled out for special mention."

Pete gazed at the floor. He had washed it three days ago but it was dirty. Neb was not cattle.

"Brother Peter, you are a good worker," Father Gabriel went on. "Maybe you have a calling. Maybe not. Brother Louis has taken vows. You have taken none. You will need to choose. We all have our choices. You have been with us for two years now. You must remember that simply in being here, you have taken a vow of obedience. Our lives here are a great mystery. We all add up to something and nobody knows what it is, but it is greater than any one of us by ourselves." He yawned. His nose looked like a strawberry. It was bright red with pores like seeds. "Nobody knows where the journey ends," he mumbled. He ordered Pete to do three Hail Marys. He rubbed his hands together and then he waved Pete away.

Were you called here? That was the question Pete asked himself when he was alone in his cell. Through his window was a view of the valley. Every day it was drenched in sunlight. The open sky spread out above. At night it filled with stars. To see the world's beauty all he had to do was look. If he leaned out, he could glimpse the roof of the barn where Neb was, and the gate beyond. But the window was not his, nothing belonged to him. That was as it should be. Other valleys lay in shadow.

2

For a long time Father Gabriel's drinking had given his sermons a light-hearted air. He read from the Book of Psalms or the Song of Songs and giggled and blushed from time to time. Every so often came a dry day, when his manner turned gruff and he took to Leviticus. He seemed to find it calming. So much of that book was plain common sense. Who needed to be told to wash the blood out of clothes, or that something became unclean if a dead body fell on it? What sort of creature would desire most of what was forbidden anyway? Only one line warned against strong wine. True, that was on pain of death, but there were whole pages against eating animal fat. Besides, drink was only frowned on in the meeting tent, the book said. So the path to virtue seemed easy to tread. Keep your things clear of falling corpses and stay out of tents. With such logic, it was no time at all before Father Gabriel's good humor was restored.

But things were changing. The bad days came more often. Even after a nip or two, Father Gabriel's mood was still dark. It was hard to tell the difference between when he was talking about heaven and when he was talking about hell. His sermons grew less considered. He seemed to be making them up as he went along. He would start by saying, "What prittle-prattle should we go on about today?" Even though he did not seem interested in what he was saying himself, he demanded full attention. In better days he had overlooked fidgeting. Now the slightest twitch among his listeners stopped him cold, and he would glare at the offender until all motion ceased. As a result, services went on twice as long as before. This in turn doubled the chance of sneezes or yawns, which sent Father Gabriel into a rage, which meant even more time. It was a vicious circle.

Brother Walter took the brunt of it. He was nervous and restless by nature. Even in the best of times he had trouble sitting still for long. To make matters worse, he had hay fever in every season and a terrible fear and hatred of ants. He understood that he was supposed to love all creation, and he thought he managed this as well as possible. But he could not pretend to love the ants. He loathed them. They seemed drawn to him, though. They were always crawling all over him at the most awkward moments. The minute he felt the telltale prickle on his skin he flew into a fit. He couldn't help it. He'd leap and moan and flap his arms, his robe flying, and he'd run up and down the halls screaming, or roll on the floor rubbing at himself until he was sure the ants were gone. Afterward, there were never any traces of them, and some of Walter's less generous brothers had been heard to doubt that they were ever there in the first place. But since these fits happened many times a week, everyone had gotten used to them. Whether during meals or in prayer or at work, Brother Walter might jump up and go into one of his mad jigs, or hurl himself to the floor and wriggle about, or go tearing past in a frenzy at any minute, and nobody would bat an eye.

Father Gabriel too had taken all this in stride in the past, but no more. Now Brother Walter sat in fear near the entryway at the back of the church, his head bowed. This was a suitable posture for the occasion, and he hoped everyone thought he was praying. What he was really doing was scanning the ground around him for ants. He thought if he saw them coming he could squish them underfoot, without moving too much, before they started crawling up his leg. So far it was working. He had not detected any ants, but neither had he jumped up screaming during mass, not for days.

This was a relief because the last time, Father Gabriel had become so furious that he had taken several names in vain and pounded on the altar so hard that a chalice fell off.

There was still the matter of Brother Walter's hay fever. To keep from sneezing, he held his breath most of the time Father Gabriel spoke. By the end he felt very light in the head, but he found he could get through it. It must have added up, though. Day by day, the dizzy feeling got worse, until one morning, as soon as the sermon began, Brother Walter saw swarms of little stars flickering in front of his eyes. Before he could take a breath, he was out cold. He slumped from his pew. Everyone turned to look. At the front of the church, Father Gabriel stopped in his tracks, anger bursting in his face. They all waited for the fit to start, but Brother Walter just lay there in the entry where he had fallen, stretched out across the floor, still as any stone. Father Gabriel cleared his throat. "Brother Walter," he said, "this is a definite improvement. However, it is still a disruption. Therefore, I find fault in you. Ten Hail Marys."

3

They met to discuss what was happening and what they should do about it. Deciding on courses of action was not their strong suit as a group. They talked for months about what two kinds of juice to keep in the pantry and could not come to an agreement. One of them thought orange juice had too much acid and was bad for the stomach. Another pointed out the benefits of cranberry. Most could not be satisfied, and the debate went on until Brother Frederic spoke up. He took it as his job to remind them of where and who they were. "A little luxury is a dangerous thing," he said. "Poverty is best for the soul." A hush fell. If Pete had not known better, he might have supposed it was a humble silence, accepting of this scolding. But he did know better, and the next week there were thirteen kinds of juice to choose from.

Pete was only invited to meetings about matters of general interest. He was not allowed to vote. Sometimes he was allowed to speak. They argued about whether he should be allowed to speak this time. Someone suggested they put it to a vote. Someone else said that was beneath them. They voted on whether to vote. It was a tie.

"But he doesn't know the history," said Brother Matthew.

"What is the history?" asked Pete.

"Don't be rude," said Brother Matthew. He had a permanent squint that gave his expression a mean look, but he didn't need the look. He was mean enough without it. "You will know what it is right for you to know."

"I've seen it coming for a long time," said Brother James, the baker, who smelled of yeast and the bourbon he used in his cakes. "I knew it couldn't last forever. Father Gabriel is backsliding."

"The question is," said Brother John, "what do we do now? I've been here longer than any of you. You have no idea what it was like in those days." Brother John's hands were twisted with arthritis. He waved them in the air as he spoke. "We can't go back to that. He used to carry a skull around with him everywhere, tucked under his arm. He said it was supposed to remind us we were mortal. If anyone looked at him cross-eyed he'd conk them on the head with it. He made us whip ourselves every night to keep us humble and he checked for the marks every day. If he didn't find any, he'd take the strap to us himself."

Brother Walter screamed and hopped on the table and began running in place.

"These last years have been paradise," Brother John went on. "Such freedom!"

"Because he was drunk all the time," said Pete. "That's no solution."

"Brother Peter, I don't believe it has been decided whether your voice will be heard," said Brother Matthew.

"Oh, let him talk," said Brother Walter, a little out of breath. It had been a brief fit. He climbed off the table and took his seat.

"It was a fine idea while it lasted," said Brother James with a sigh, "but now he has built up a tolerance. We should be thankful it took this long. The drink doesn't keep him happy any more, that's all there is to it. We'll have to think of something else."

"A fine idea?" said Pete. "Do you mean to say you *gave* him the liquor?"

"A little with his coffee at first, perhaps, until the seed was planted. There was twice as much every week as I needed for my cakes. He wasn't one to turn it down. It was so good for his temper, we let it be known we would look the other way."

Brother Dominic sat in a corner filing his fingernails. His eyes were as calm and blue as a dove. He did not look at Pete when they were among others. If he had anything to say, he kept it to himself.

It was agreed that this was a more complicated question than that of the juice. It could not be resolved in a single session. As the meeting came to a close, Pete spoke up again. "He needs help," he said. "Father Gabriel needs help."

This gave Brother Frederic his chance to chime in. "The Lord helps those who help themselves," he said.

4

They took their meals in silence, side by side at tables for two, each one facing the crucifix at the front of the room. One day Pete felt Brother Dominic's knee pressing against his under the table. He thought it had gone on too long to be an accident, but he couldn't be sure until Brother Dominic came to his door after midnight. He kept coming every week or two. It did not feel like sin. Brother Dominic never sat at his table again. There was no way of knowing when he would appear at night, or when he would not. Once there was a commotion in the hall outside Pete's cell and they thought they had been found out, but it was only Brother Walter streaking past.

Brother Dominic had a right to be vain, and he was. He had been a movie star as a teenager, playing a boy genius in a series of popular films two decades before. Years of drug abuse followed, but he looked no worse for the wear. He seemed vexed that Pete had never heard of him, but his disappointment was short-lived. Pete tried to make him feel better by telling him that anyone could see he was still handsome enough to be a movie star. In fact, the word Pete used was *beautiful*. Brother Dominic ignored him. The only compliments he accepted were the ones he paid himself.

They did not talk much, but when they did, no matter what the subject, Brother Dominic brought it back to his past career.

"I feel like I've been waiting for something my whole life," Pete remarked one night, in a philosophical mood. "But I don't know what it is."

"Try working in Hollywood," said Brother Dominic. "An hour a day in front of the camera and the rest of the time sitting around your dressing room waiting for your call. Now that's waiting."

This sort of thing made him difficult to talk to.

They were what Pete had been running from, these feelings, yet here they were again. He should have been more afraid of them here, for if they followed him here, even here, it must mean they would never go away. But somehow he was less afraid, not more. He even got up the courage, one night as Brother Dominic was leaving, to ask, “Do you love me?”

Brother Dominic finished pulling his robe over his head and stood staring into what would have been a great distance, if the walls of Pete’s little cell had not closed it off. Finally he answered. “Whatever gave you that idea?”

That was when Pete knew he would have to return to the world.

5

As a boy, Pete thought his faith had saved him, but if anyone had asked what it saved him from, he would not have known how to answer. Nobody ever asked. He grew up in a mansion on a hill overlooking the bay. His father was often away on business and his mother was cheerful and vague. She was never without a smile even though most things appeared to puzzle her. Whenever she caught sight of Pete, she looked surprised. "Oh, there you are!" she would cry, as if she thought he'd been lost, even when he had been there all along.

Pete's father called his banker every morning to find out how much money he had to spend that day. Then he spent it all before nightfall. By the time he was ten, Pete understood that not everyone lived this way. He knew it meant his parents were not true believers. Nobody was. If they were, they would sell what they had and give the money to the poor. If they were, they would not be hunched at mass like tired workers, murmuring under their breath. They would stand and sing.

The world would be a different place.

But the world was what it was. Pete had nothing to sell. None of it was his, and he was glad. He learned to live among the trappings of prosperity while always looking beyond to the true splendors of divinity. His father noted a certain absence about him. “Damn it, boy, where’s your head?” he yelled.

When Pete became an altar boy, his father told him to beware of the priests. “Don’t you ever let them get the better of you,” he said. Pete had no idea what he was talking about. The priests were less godly than Pete had hoped. They dozed off when they should have been mindful. Many were unkind. One of them always had a head cold. They were all very human. Everyone was. That was all they had going for them, and Pete was supposed to love them for it.

“That boy is just like his mother,” Pete heard his father telling his friends. “Always with his head in the clouds.” They decided to send him to a boarding school where religion was kept in the proper perspective. Maybe that would break him, his father said. Pete begged his mother not to send him. She only smiled and shook her head and turned away.

The feelings were already there by the time he left. It seemed they always had been. At school he met a boy named Michael who wore big glasses that gave him the look of an owl. Michael read philosophy and poetry and said it proved there was no other life than this one, and this one wasn't all it was cracked up to be. They talked and played chess, together all the time. One afternoon Michael grabbed Pete by the arm and they fell across the chessboard, rolling on the scattered pieces. One way to worship, and to cast off selfishness, was in overwhelming love for another human being. Pete knew that. What scared him, apart from everything else, was that he had never felt more like himself before.

His father must have got wind of this friendship, because when Pete went home for holidays all his father talked about were queers. The house was always filled with company, and they all sat and listened, nodding as he ranted. "It's bad parenting," he said. "Do you think anyone would turn out queer if they had the right discipline? You beat it out of them, that's all. No kid of mine, I'll tell you that. They'd know better. You can bet your bottom dollar. They'd know I wouldn't stand for it. I'd run them off. I'd run off the whole damn brood!"

What brood? thought Pete. He was the only one.

When his glasses came off, Michael was beautiful. His eyes were clear and steady. They seemed to see everything without having to judge it. His eyebrows were smooth and soft, a shade darker than his soft blond hair. If there was beauty, Pete thought, that was where it could be found, underneath. But some time later it struck him that Michael was beautiful with his glasses on, too.

Pete and Michael decided to run away together. They would hitchhike south to where it was warmer, because they thought they would have to live on the streets for a while. Before they could leave, Pete was called to the headmaster's office and told he was being sent to a different school. He had an hour to pack. He couldn't find Michael. He sent him letters from the new school, but he could not be sure they were ever delivered. No answers came.

He had only a year left of school. He spent it reading scripture. He had more questions than before, and he wanted them answered more than ever.

It had been a military school so it was natural that he go from there into the army. When he was home on leave, his father clapped him on the back and told him he was proud of him.

"You spend your life cheating people," said Pete, "and you call it business."

His father turned pale with rage. "That's it," he said. "That's the end."

Pete was no more surprised than his

father was when he was discharged after two years. The only surprise was that it had taken so long. He moved to the city where he and Michael had planned to live together, and he got a job in a shopping mall. He sat in a back room watching the video screens, looking for shoplifters. What he saw stunned him. All the lost souls, all the lonely and desperate, wandering by, across these screens. It was amazing what people would do when they thought no one was looking. But why should they ever think so?

There was a divinity school nearby. Some of the teachers allowed Pete to sit in on their classes. He heard there about a place in the hills where he could go for a retreat. He sent a letter to Father Gabriel. "I feel like I have been waiting for something all my life," he wrote. "And now I think I know what it is."

Father Gabriel read the letter late one night by the dim light of the lamp at his desk. He could not accept just anyone, but it had been years since he had turned anyone away. That was mostly because so few came. It was a different world, and from what he heard, Father Gabriel was glad to be out of it. Still, something about the letter wrenched his heart. He knew nothing about the writer, this Pete, but he knew the type. Only a boy, and with nowhere else to go.

6

Pete brought Father Gabriel his tea.

"What's this?" asked Father Gabriel.

"It's your tea, Father."

Father Gabriel slammed shut the thick book on his desk. A wisp of dust puffed up from it. "So," he said, "now you're in on it too!" He had begun using words like "it" and "they" with little sense of what the words referred to. "They're poisoning the water," said Father Gabriel. "I won't drink it."

"But Father, nobody can do without water."

"I can do without anything."

Sometimes "they" meant Hindus. Father Gabriel had become convinced that the Hindus were trying to make everyone else look bad. He professed this belief in his sermons. "They think they're so all-fire holy," he said with a sneer, "living on nothing but a few grains of rice and some orange seeds. And when they get old they go off with nothing but a begging bowl and sit by the side of the road until the cows come home. God wants us to do with little in this world, yes, but he does not ask us to be bums and hobos. But what do they know of God–they, who do not believe in one God? They think birds are gods. Imagine–birds! And what do you expect from people who think it makes them holy to go around without shoes? Their clothing consists of nothing but turbans and little swatches of fabric they throw over themselves that might slip off at any minute. That's not being modest, it's being pagan. What else would you call it–the gurus with their devil smiles, and the wild dances with the drums and the pipes and the snake-charmers. It's pagan, I tell you."

Father Gabriel's behavior grew stranger by the day. His ill tempers gave way to bouts of joy, then shifted back again. During the happy periods, one would often find him trying to stand on his head. Whether dark or light of mood, he paced back and forth without stopping, even when he was presiding over services. He ran up and down the stairs to the steeple at odd hours and swung with glee on the ropes that rang the bells.

Pete found Brother James in the bakery. "Can't you see I'm busy?" said

Brother James. "These cakes bring in money. You might think they're nothing, but if it weren't for my cakes you would starve."

"Father Gabriel thinks you're putting something in the water," said Pete. "I would like to tell him that is not true."

"Thank you for your concern, Brother Peter. You may rest assured that matters are in hand."

"I know you have all been meeting without me. What are you up to?"

"How dare you speak to me in this way. You will have to answer for it. Don't think you won't."

7

Neb was Pete's great comfort. He spent as much time as he could in the barn, brushing her coat. She accepted all and wanted nothing. She brought him such peace. Her stillness was beautiful. The only real love was the love that was not given or taken. It just was, without condition. He hoped he loved her with no thought of the peace she gave him. But even when he prayed, he felt he was demanding something. Give me devotion, give me knowledge, make me see. Neb demanded nothing.

Her eyes were clear and dark and steady. Pete knew she saw him truly even though she seemed always to be looking beyond things, never at them. That was her way of being present, and she was only present, thought Pete. She had no past.

Only when he forgot that she liked to stand in the doorway while he was with her would she nudge him and tilt her graceful head. It was the gentlest of demands. Then he would let her out of her stall and lead her forward to where she could feel the breeze. She loved how it ruffled her mane, even when the wind was hot.

He stayed with her until they heard the bells calling him away.

8

Soon after dark one night, Pete was lying in his cell when he heard someone whistling. He rose and went to the window. The moon was out, so he could see that there was a figure standing at the gate. He stood in a pale moonbeam but his face was wreathed in darkness. Even so, the whites of his eyes shone through, as bright as stars. His whistle came in short, tuneless bursts, a few loose notes and then a long silence, over and over. It was no song Pete could name. After a long while, the man lit a cigarette. When he struck the match, Pete saw his face in the light of the flame. He wore a full black beard, and his hair was long and tangled. As he drew on the cigarette, Pete heard the rattle of his breath carrying across the distance. Pete shivered.

The next day the man came into the church just as Father Gabriel was beginning to speak. He wore overalls and soiled white sneakers, one of them unlaced. He sauntered in front of the altar, facing the assembly, and put his finger to his lips, making a long, quiet shushing noise. “What is this?” roared Father Gabriel. “Who in blazes are you?”

The man did not turn to look at him. “I am the saint with no name,” he said, “but you can call me Amos. I have come very far, from the other edge of the land. It is the eighth day of the ninth month of the tenth year, and I bring you news of the world. But not the one you can see. I bring you news of the *real* world.”

"Why do you all just sit there?" Father Gabriel thumped on the altar. "Somebody do something!"

"I do not set my face against you," the stranger went on. "The revealed Word is not easy to hear but it will save us all. Follow me." He walked slowly to the door and went out.

"Did he mean we were supposed to go after him?" Brother Walter asked meekly.

"Shut your gob, you simpleton," howled Father Gabriel. "Who let this madman in? Do you think we can have crazy people coming in and out, on top of everything else? I will get to the bottom of this if it's the last thing I do."

"I found him sleeping in the bakery this morning," said Brother James. "He told me he was hungry. I gave him food. We deal in charity here, Father."

"Don't talk to me about charity. The man is a loon. I can't help it if everything's gone to hell in a handbasket, but I'll be damned if we will give refuge to a maniac. I am calling in the authorities."

"Do you think that's wise, Father?"

"I will be the judge of what is wise, Brother James."

9

Two police officers arrived half an hour later. "What took you so long?" Father Gabriel demanded. One of the officers was a tall man with a single thick eyebrow cutting across his forehead from side to side. The other was a small woman with oversized pants that flared out at her hips. Her cap was perched at an angle on her bunched-up hair. Both looked uneasy.

"You didn't say it was an emergency," said the man. "I got the papers right here. It don't say anything about an emergency."

"Of course it's an emergency," snapped Father Gabriel. "We have had an intruder. If the place were burning to the ground would you need to be told it was urgent?"

The officer blinked at his notebook. "I don't see nothing here about a fire," he said. "Let's not get ahead of ourselves. First things first. I am Officer Stingo and this here is Officer Lund." Officer Lund put her hand on top of her cap to hold it in place as she nodded. "We're here to check into your complaint. Now, you say there was an intruder?"

"Yes, yes."

"And what exactly was it that this intruder done?"

Father Gabriel closed his eyes and let out a long breath. "Intruded," he said.

"Was this alleged intruder of the male or female gender?"

"It was a man–a crazy man who came

out of nowhere and walked right in here without so much as a by-your-leave."

Officer Stingo scratched his cheek with his pen and then scrawled something down on his pad. "Men don't come out of nowhere, sir," he said. "That's one thing you can be sure of. Now, you're telling me this alleged male intruder was uninvited?"

Officer Lund was slowly circling the foyer, inspecting the location, her hand on her cap as she looked up at the rafters or down at the hardwood floor. Father Gabriel watched her with narrow eyes. "Yes, the intruder was uninvited," he said. "You could say that is the essence of what made him an intruder."

"And how exactly would you describe this alleged male intruder, sir?"

"I already told you. He was crazy. What the devil is she doing?" Officer Lund was crouched down, poking at the floor.

"Loose plank, sir," she said. "Someone might trip."

"I'll see to it promptly," said Father Gabriel, but his sarcasm seemed to be lost on them.

"Is there anything under this floor, sir?"

"Yes. The ground."

"You shouldn't take these things lightly, sir. Some of these intruders are sly ones. You never know where they might be hiding out. Now, I believe you were about to describe him."

Brother James stepped forward from the group that stood watching from the hall. He was holding his rosary. It dangled before him from his clasped hands. The silver crucifix glinted. "He had a glow," said Brother James. "He had a heavenly glow. It was like he was lit from within. His skin was the purest of the pure, like … alabaster."

Officer Stingo nodded. "Male Caucasian," he said, jotting it down.

"And his eyes," added Brother John, his voice thick and trembling. "His eyes blazed. They pierced right through you but bathed you in their warmth."

"Color?" asked Officer Stingo.

"They had no earthly color," said Brother John. "They were not of this world."

Uncertain what to record in response to this, Officer Stingo tapped the pen against the pad and squinted. Brother Walter screamed, hopped, flailed his arms, and ran off down the hall.

"Who was that?" asked Officer Stingo. "Seems suspicious."

"Never mind about him," said Father Gabriel. "I want to know what has gotten into everybody. You all talk about this stranger as if he were some sort of a prophet."

"He said he was a saint," said Brother James, drawing his clasped hands to his chin, "and I believed him."

Father Gabriel gasped. "Have you taken leave of your senses?"

"Where is this saint now, sir?" asked Officer Stingo.

"He's not a saint, damn it all–and by this time he could be in the next county for all I know, even if he was going by ox-cart!"

Officer Lund approached Brother Dominic, staring into his face. "Don't I know you from someplace?" she asked.

Brother Dominic batted his eyes. "I used to be in pictures," he said.

"It *is* you." Officer Lund clapped her hand to her heart. "Morty McGrew, Boy Genius! I've loved you since I was a kid. Will you sign my field book?"

"Oh, for the love of God," cried Father Gabriel.

Officer Stingo placed his pen to his pad, poised to write. "Could you describe this ox-cart, sir?" he asked.

The officers searched the abbey and the grounds with Father Gabriel following them, waving his arms and shouting instructions that they ignored. They covered the yard and searched the barn. "Loose planks back here too, sir," said Officer Lund, tapping at the wall behind the trough. "Oh, get on with it, get on with it!" said Father Gabriel. They looked inside cabinets and under pews, into teapots and holy vessels. They opened the door of every cell and searched under every bed. No sign of an intruder was found.

But he was still there somewhere, Pete was sure of it. At first it was only a feeling. Then there were signs. The next day, after he washed the kitchen floor and was starting on the refectory, he heard a clanging sound behind him. He hurried back to the kitchen and found footprints tracking across the wet floor, leading out the rear door. The footprints were shaped like two half moons with curlicue patterns of circles and lines. At night he heard a stirring outside his cell. At first he thought it might be Brother Dominic, but there was no knock, and then he caught a whiff of smoke. He hurried to the door and peered into the hall. It was empty. But it was the strange kind of emptiness left behind in the split second after someone had just been there.

That was a kind of emptiness Pete knew. All his life he had been aware of it. If his faith was true, it meant there was a hidden presence in everything. As a boy he thought if he looked hard enough, he would be able to see it. As he grew, he knew this was wrong. Faith meant not needing to see. The presence was there but escaped ordinary senses. Then Pete lived in a constant state of almost seeing. Every place was like a room where a bright light had just gone off. Always, Pete felt he could almost see what was left of that light, which still burned elsewhere. It made everything he looked at seem fleeting, like passing birds glimpsed from the corner of the eye. He scanned the world's surface and thought it was like staring into a big blank sky filled with beautiful clouds that were too high, or too deep, or too far away to be evident. To believe they were there all the same was the only way he knew to find that the world was not empty.

The footprints he had seen in the kitchen, thought Pete, were exactly the kind a sneaker would leave.

10

Everything appeared to return to normal, for what that was worth. If anything, things got better. The brothers were all in high spirits. Even Brother James and Brother Matthew greeted Pete with good cheer as they passed. At choir, everyone sang in clear and faithful voices. Days went by in which Brother Walter had no run-ins with the ants. Brother John's twisted hands straightened out a little, and Brother Frederic's sayings tended a bit more toward the New Testament. All the while, there were odd comings and goings, and Pete had no idea what it all meant.

Father Gabriel took to his room. Hours of prayer went on as usual, though with few in attendance. Pete went into the church for the afternoon mass to find no one there but Brother Louis, who was kneeling at a front pew. Pete had not seen him since that day on the hill. He looked up at the ceiling when he heard Pete come in. Pete knew there was no point in asking him where everybody was. Even if he were not under a vow of silence, Brother Louis would not waste his breath on Pete.

Brother Louis drew himself up and slowly walked with his head bowed to where Pete stood in the back. His footsteps on the hard floor echoed. He stood beside Pete without looking at him.

"I don't have anything against you," said Pete, "as long as you leave Neb alone."

Brother Louis kept his head bowed. His eyes were steely and calm. His breathing was heavy, and his nostrils flared. He stood stock-still for a long moment. Then he raised his arm and swept it to his side. It caught Pete by the shoulder and knocked him down. He hit the hard edge of a pew and then fell to the ground. Without turning to look down at Pete, Brother Louis stalked out.

11

By the light of a candle, Pete was looking in a mirror at the bruises on his side that night when Brother Dominic knocked. "What happened to you?" Brother Dominic asked when he saw the bruises. "I've got some makeup for that if you want it. A solid foundation and then a little light cover work, brushed in just right. You'd be amazed."

"We have to talk," said Pete.

"I've been thinking the same thing." Brother Dominic sat on the bed and put his hands on his knees. "I've been thinking about what you asked me and there's something I need to tell you. I'm not really, you know, gay."

"That isn't what I had in mind."

"You don't understand," Brother Dominic went on. "You have no idea what it was like. No one does. Just a kid, thrown into the spotlight, living in the fast lane. It was all too much. It's a whole other world. There's no gay or straight there, it's all just, like, anything goes. Believe me, I could tell you stories. Do you see what I'm saying? Everything's different in Hollywood."

"We're not in Hollywood," said Pete. "But that's not what I'm talking about. That's all over. I want to know if you have seen him. You know what I mean."

Brother Dominic closed his mouth and took a breath, his face turned down in the flickering light. He nodded. "He came to me alone," he said. "I was working in the sacristy. You know how I hate to use that awful polish that smells like vinegar? Well, suddenly the smell turned sweet and a light came on, and everything was changed, and he was there. He said he was the saint with no name but I should call him Amos. He told me we are at a great crossroads and he has come to lead us. Then he told me to meet him that night in the woods."

"And you did."

"Everyone was there. He'd come to each of us alone, one by one, the very same way, to tell us where and when to meet him. He said there were three crimes and there would be a fourth and the fourth would be in fire. He said if we followed the road we were on then our pastures would languish. I didn't really get that part. Then he said there would be no rain for a long time. That seemed like a no-brainer because it never rains around here anyway, but whatever. But then he said something that really grabbed me. He said, 'Do not go with the ones that sell the just man for silver.' And I was like: *yes*. It was like he was talking about me! They never cared about me, all those money-men, all they cared about was the bottom line. It was always just Morty McGrew this and Morty McGrew that–never about me as a *person*. One of the papers said it was because my agent dumped me but that was the real reason I got out of the business."

Pete sat next to Brother Dominic and put a hand on his shoulder. "This is hopeless," he said. "It's all so hopeless."

Brother Dominic looked at him, his eyes reflecting the candle's flame. "He'll come to you, too," he said. "Then you'll see."

12

Pete found himself waiting again. Now he knew what he was waiting for, but he did not know what he would do when it came.

He knocked on Father Gabriel's door. "Go away!" came a shout from within.

"It's me, Father."

"I don't care if it's the Second Coming. I have a toothache. Go away."

It was in the barn that the stranger came to him.

Pete was watching Neb drink and singing to her. He held the bucket for her and stroked her neck as she lapped at the water with her big pink tongue. She seemed thirstier than usual, and Pete thought there was a sad look in her eyes before he began to sing. When he brushed her, he saw what was wrong. Across her haunches were many long red gashes. Dried blood streaked down her legs. Someone had whipped her.

A little water was left in the bucket. Pete poured it over her. It trickled across her wounds. Pete wiped the blood away. It covered his own hands. He sat in the straw and wept. Neb stirred and tried to twist her neck so she could see him behind her, but she was tied to a beam, and it was impossible. He needed comfort, but she could not turn. There were so many things a donkey's body could not do. She lowered her head.

A shadow loomed over Pete and he looked up to see the stranger standing in the doorway. "What are you crying for?" the stranger asked.

Pete wiped his eyes, smearing blood across his face. "Brother Louis beat Neb," he said.

"Tough world," said the stranger. He coughed against the back of his fist. "Don't sound like no brother of mine." With a slight stagger, he crossed the barn to a stool against the wall. He sank down onto the stool so heavily it nearly tipped over.

Pete had been the first to see him the night he came. He had not been this close until now. Now the man looked small and harmless, crouched on his stool with tired eyes. "I feel like I've seen you somewhere," said Pete.

"Some say I look like Santy Claus in reverse," said the stranger. "Makes me real proud. Mind if I light up?"

"You'll set the barn on fire."

He struck a match and lit the cigarette. "I don't really need permission," he said. "I was only asking to be polite." He dropped the match in the hay and stomped on it with the toe of his sneaker.

"What are you doing here?" asked Pete.

The stranger shrugged. "Biding my time. I go here and there. Where I'm called. I'm on a mission."

"What mission is that?"

"Upheaval." He grinned, showing crooked yellow teeth. "An enemy shall surround the land and strip you of your strengths."

"Are you a prophet?"

"Depends how you mean. Do I know what's what? Yeah, I know what's what. I seen some things. I've lived a life that would break most people in two. I know which end is up."

"You told them there were three crimes and a fourth would be in fire."

The stranger inhaled the cigarette's smoke. Then he blew it out. It formed a cloud in front of his face. He leaned forward and breathed in the cloud, a long, rasping breath. Only then did he speak. "Bunch of bull," he said. "Make it up as you go along and it sounds as good as the book."

"They believe you," said Pete.

"These chumps will believe anything. Until they don't."

"But why? Why us?"

"I like to mess with people. And let's just say like a lot of people I got a little grudge against your outfit. Plus I'm, you know, evil." He grinned the yellow-toothed smile again.

That was when Pete knew why he looked familiar. He was one of the lost, akin to those people Pete had watched helplessly all those years, straggling across the video screens in the back of the shopping mall. "You're a criminal," said Pete. "You're just a common criminal."

The stranger rose to his feet so fast that this time the stool did fall over. "I'm not common," he said. Neb stepped forward, between him and Pete, and gave a warning snuffle. The stranger looked at her and then patted her head to calm her. "Or what the hell, maybe I am. Truth is, I'm just a middleman. I got my higher-ups just like you got yours, and they don't give me the time of day, just like yours. I put in my time on the streets, sure. You want to know what I do when I can get body and soul together? I deal in bliss. I sell bliss, on behalf of those higher-ups I mentioned. I sell it to the ones that don't want to put up with a lot of crap to get it. The thing about bliss is it comes in these tiny little white grains. Put them all together and they add up to the most beautiful heaps of white powder. Pure as the driven snow. A little bit of that shit and you're face to face with the frickin divine, without any of the baloney."

"I'll go to Father Gabriel," said Pete.

The stranger threw back his head and laughed. The locks of his beard shook.

"Then I'll go to the police."

"The *po*-lice! You're a funny kid with that little moral thing of yours that's worth about a plug nickel. Speaking of the *po*-lice, they could have found themselves a whole shitload of bliss around here if they knew their elbows from their assholes. Trouble with them is they're always casing out the nooks when they should be scoping out the crannies, and vice versa. But those chumps could have died and gone to copper heaven, if only they knew where to look. This place here, see, is lousy with those beautiful little heaps of pure white. One of your guys been meeting up with one of my guys–and I don't mean to dance the tango. So let's not go getting up on our high horse so right quick."

"I don't believe it," said Pete.

"That's how I come to learn about your cozy little setup out here. And then I just had to come have a look-see for myself. Didn't take long to get the lay of the land. I'm not saying your good brothers don't get some of their own now and then but mostly they been slipping it to the old geezer. Who, alas and alack, is beyond bliss, if you know what I mean."

Pete looked down at his hands, where the blood had dried. He shook his head.

It was so much worse than he had feared that he was dazed. “Why have you told me this?” he asked.

“Maybe because I got it figured they don’t listen to you. Like I said, I like to mess with people.” He patted Neb on the head again. “Or maybe it’s because you like the mule. And now if you will excuse me, I got my mission to attend to.”

13

The walls around him looked barer than ever. They were huge and thick, made of stone. They were meant to hold in the warmth of a living flame and to close out the corruptions of the world. Pete had spent his life praying for grace. He saw that this amounted to one long plea for help that never came, and might have been of little use to him if it had. Now he did not know what to pray for. The thought that he could ever have left the world behind seemed like the vainest of hopes.

When Louis came to take Neb into the valley to bring back the wood, Pete was waiting. He was hiding in the loft. Neb knew he was up there, but she was frightened all the same. Pete could tell by the way she drew back. The barn door was kept open because it jammed if it was shut, so they could both see him coming. Louis was rough in harnessing her. She wouldn't budge at first, and Louis pulled with more force. The bridle pressed hard against her jaw. She brayed a little but stepped forward. Pete watched as Louis led her from the barn. She moved with halting steps. Pete climbed out of the loft and watched from the doorway as he led her down the hill.

Louis set to work on a tree that was already fallen. He chopped the wood in hard, clean strokes and stacked the split logs in the wheelbarrow. Pete watched from behind a tree. He was surprised when he heard Louis begin to sing a hymn, the same one over and over as he worked. "I rest my weary soul in thee," he sang. "I give thee back the life I owe, that in thine ocean depths it flow, may richer, fuller be." The notes he sang heaved as he swung the axe, but the hymn was slow and peaceful. The longer he worked, the quieter his song grew.

By the time he was finished, the cart was overflowing. It was a great burden. Neb took a few steps, then stopped. The load was too heavy. She needed water to go on. She planted her hooves on the ground. The dark look came to Louis's eyes then, and the trace of a mean smile quivered his mouth. "You wicked creature," he said under his breath. "God damn you."

It was the first time Pete had heard

him speak. It was different from his singing voice, with its clear, pure tones. In speech, his voice was husky and hoarse.

Seething, Louis bent to snatch a thick branch from the ground, but by the time he stood up again, Pete was there, between him and Neb. Pete grabbed the stick from him and threw it far away into the woods. They faced each other. Then Louis turned to where the axe lay nearby. Neb let out a little whinny. Louis hoisted the axe over his shoulder and turned back to Pete.

"You broke your vow," said Pete. "I heard you."

"You lead the damned thing back then," said Louis. "It does what you tell it."

"I wouldn't beat her, even if she didn't."

"And you can store the wood too, while you're at it. Earn your keep."

"I do my work," answered Pete.

"But you don't do it for God. My work is part of my holy calling. That is why I am on this earth. I have never doubted it for an instant. I came here to find the silence that fits our souls for the divine union. At every turn something stands between me and my redeemer. I know my soul is being tested. I love God more for it. But you make a mockery of all that holds my spirit up, and that cursed animal loves you for it."

Pete cast his eyes down. There was some truth in what Louis said. Pete had seen him at work. He saw that work was, for Louis, a part of something sacred. "It's only that I'm kind to her," he said.

"God wills us to be kind when we see His spirit in the world. But woe to those who turn judgment to wormwood. In every street they shall cry. I am condemned to live this life among fools and sinners. A silly old goat who drowns himself in drink. A lot of rogues who do dirt on all the hosts of heaven but throw themselves at the feet of false idols. And I am bitter. I am sorely bitter in my thoughts."

"Be bitter then," said Pete. "But this is the last time you will ever lay a hand on Neb."

"I am bitter in my thoughts. But I am not bitter in my soul. And it is from my soul that I act. All that I do is in the name of God, who made the dawn and the darkness. This is nothing you can understand–you, with your blubbering doubts that you've tried to weave into a faith. I am not so afflicted." Louis went to the cart and dropped the axe on top of the stacked wood. "What I do is good because I do it." Then he wiped his hands together and started up the hill.

14

Pete stood at Father Gabriel's door. This time he would not be put off. He heard Father Gabriel moaning from within. Then he heard the bolt turn. As Pete entered, he saw Father Gabriel climbing back into bed. He burrowed under the covers, head first, his bare feet sticking out. "Oh, my tooth is killing me," he said.

"We are in crisis, Father," said Pete. "You have to do something."

"I'm being punished," said Father Gabriel. "This is my punishment, and I deserve it."

"A toothache is a very small thing, Father."

"Don't lecture me, you knave. I'm not talking about my toothache. That is bad enough, and you are in no position to speak of it." Kicking his legs, he crawled forward until his head poked out from under the blankets. His hair was gnarled and matted, and his eyes were watery. "I have heard from the superiors. They are not pleased. They found out the police were called, and they don't like it. All these years they paid no attention. They forgot we were here. That was our only hope. Now they are coming to see the state of things, and that will be the end of it. They'll shut us down."

Pete sat at the foot of the bed. "Maybe they won't," he said. But maybe it would be for the best, he thought.

"That's not the worst of it." Father

Gabriel pulled a pillow out from under him and hugged it, squeezing it to his chest. “They have given me a task. I am to preside at the funeral of the unknowns.” He shuddered. “It’s a burial service for those whose remains have not been claimed. Everyone lines up at the graveside, one poor sod from each church just to be on the safe side because they don’t know what the dead people were. Probably they were heathen but never mind. Then you mutter a few words while they put the ashes in the ground. Oh, how depressing it all is. I’ll have to stand there like a muggins, alongside a Protestant and who knows what else. Probably a Hindu for all I know.”

“Won’t it be a comfort?” Pete suggested. “To go back to doing good works, I mean.”

“Good works,” Father Gabriel scoffed. He flung the pillow against the wall. “It is not an honor. Far from it. They only make the flunkies do it–the ones who are on their way out. It’s the last stop on the crap-out train, and I’ve got a one-way ticket.”

“If it won’t comfort you, won’t it help to know that it might comfort others?”

Father Gabriel glared at him. “I don’t know why you go on like this. It only makes you ridiculous.” He drew himself up. “Oh well, if it’s not one kind of poison it’s another. I had better gird my loins. Bring the car around.”

15

The old Jeep made its way down the mountain toward the village, with Pete at the wheel and Father Gabriel beside him. The engine made terrible grinding noises and the seats creaked as the truck bumped along. The sun was brilliant and the sky a deep, deep blue. It had been a long time since Pete had gone this far into the world, and everything looked strange and dazzling. He was afraid he would not remember how to drive and was pleased at how it all came back to him. Father Gabriel pulled a flask from out of his vest and took a swig from it. "My tooth is killing me," he said. "This is for the pain. After this is over I will never have another drop. So don't say a word."

"I won't," said Pete.

They drove through the village with its large frame houses and its tree-shaded roads, nearer to the city, where the sun was harsher and the streets were wide and cracked, skirted with liquor stores and pawnshops and bail bonds offices. The graveyard was just off a busy avenue. The plot they were directed to was in a far corner on a little rise backed up against a high fence. Beyond the fence was a tall concrete wall. It was a highway overpass. Traffic rasped and bleated above. The grave lay under a stand of sickly palm trees. A few people in black stood around it. "This is grim," said Father Gabriel, hunching down in the creaking seat as

Pete parked the Jeep. “Oh, it’s worse than my worst nightmares.”

A man holding a clipboard with a pencil behind his ear greeted them. He wore a red tie and a light blue short-sleeved shirt. “Thanks for coming, Father,” he said. “You’re the only one. Nobody else showed.” He shrugged. “I’m from the county. We can start whenever you’re ready.”

“Who are all those other people?” asked Father Gabriel.

“Them? Well, a couple of them knew one or another of the deceased, as far as I can tell. Most just like to go to funerals, I guess. The ones we’re putting in didn’t have much in the way of kin.”

“How many are there?”

“Of the deceased, you mean?” The

man looked at his clipboard. "That would be fourteen hundred, Father."

"How's that again?"

"That would be fourteen hundred."

"Do you mean to say one thousand and four hundred?"

"One thousand four hundred and fifty-six, to be exact," the man answered, consulting the clipboard again. "It's about a year's worth."

"Excuse me please," said Father Gabriel.

He turned and walked back to the Jeep. Pete and the man from the county watched him go. His steps were unhurried, and he looked around him as he walked as if he were out for a stroll. He opened the Jeep's door carefully. Then he lurched into the front seat, slamming the door behind him. He stared ahead for several minutes. Then he put his head down and covered his face with his hands. Pete saw his shoulders start to heave.

The man from the county took the pencil from behind his ear and scratched his nose with the eraser end. "Do you think he'll be back?" he asked Pete.

"I think so," Pete answered. "I think he will."

The man shrugged again. He pulled a stick of gum out of his pocket, unwrapped it, and folded it into his mouth. He rolled the foil wrapper into a little silver ball and played it between his fingers.

A few minutes later, Father Gabriel got out of the Jeep. He walked past Pete without looking at him and took his place beside the open grave. It was filled with a mound of black plastic bags. They were tied shut with yellow bands. Many were dusted with streaks of gray-white ash.

Father Gabriel clasped his hands together and, looking downward, began to speak. "God did not make death. Nor does He rejoice in the destruction of the living. He fashioned all things that they might have being, and the creatures of the world are wholesome. There is not a destructive drug among them, nor any domain of the nether world on earth, for justice is undying. This is a reading from the Book of Wisdom."

There was a pause. Father Gabriel raised his eyebrows at the scattered mourners. "Amen," a few of them murmured.

"The breakers of death surged round about me," he went on. "The floods of perdition overwhelmed me. In my distress I called upon the Lord. From His temple, He heard my voice, and my cry reached His ears."

After he was finished speaking, Father Gabriel nodded and strode away, back to where Pete stood. He closed his hand around Pete's arm and held it there. Pete felt his hand tremble.

"Thanks, Father," said the man from the county, chewing his gum. "That was great."

"Do you know a cheap dentist?" asked Father Gabriel.

"Sure, there's a clinic right here

in Pomona. I'll write down the directions."

A mourner made her way toward them. One of her shoes was much bigger than the other, and she walked with a limp, holding up a black umbrella that was open above her to block the sun. She gazed at Father Gabriel through the black mesh of her veil. "My brother's in there," she said, tilting the umbrella toward the grave. "My little brother Kenny. He never come to much but I wisht it hadn't ended up this way."

"Your brother is not there, my child," said Father Gabriel. "His soul is with God."

"Do you think so, Father?" She leaned forward hopefully. Her eyes glistened.

"Do you really think so? He could never catch a break. They got him on every little thing. He tried and tried but it was just no use. Nothing ever come out right. He was a lot younger than me. I used to play with him when he was just a baby. He was such a little baby. But he never had a chance." Her voice broke, and she sobbed. "That poor boy just never had a chance."

"There, there," said Father Gabriel. He tightened his grip on Pete's arm. "God's way is unerring. He is a shield for all who take refuge in him."

The woman shut her eyes tightly. Then she opened them wide. A tear dropped to her cheek. "Thank you, Father," she said. "Oh, thank you, thank you."

Father Gabriel nodded, turned to Pete, and snarled under his breath, "Get me out of here."

In the Jeep, Pete said, "You gave that woman comfort."

"Drive faster," said Father Gabriel. "My tooth is killing me."

"I'm going the speed limit."

"It was Samuel. The Book of Samuel. The verse goes on from there. 'They cried for help, but no one saved them– to the Lord, but he answered them not. I ground them fine as the dust of the earth. Like the mud in the streets I trampled them down.'"

16

The dentist's office was in a little strip mall between a car wash and a trailer park. On the plate glass window in front was a picture of a big white tooth with a smiling face. When they got out of the Jeep, Father Gabriel took hold of Pete's arm again and did not let go. The waiting room was mostly full. A nurse at the desk told them to take a seat. Father Gabriel glanced around the room. "Look at them all," he muttered to Pete. "Just look at them. This time next year they'll all be ash and I'll be yammering over their grave." The woman sitting next to him got up and moved to another chair.

When the nurse called him in, Father Gabriel insisted Pete come with him.

As they entered Father Gabriel stopped short when he saw an Indian man in a green smock standing inside. "Are you the doctor?"

"I am that," the man answered with a chuckle.

"It's a Hindu," Father Gabriel gasped, still clutching Pete's arm. "You have brought me to a Hindu!"

"I am pleased to say I am a nonbeliever," the doctor said. "Do come in."

Father Gabriel settled uneasily into the chair. The doctor pressed a button, and the chair slanted backward with a low buzzing sound. "What's happening? What are you doing?" Father Gabriel clutched at the chair's arms.

"The better to see you with," chuckled the doctor, sitting on a stool beside the chair. "Now, open wide. Oh my. Have you been drinking?"

"What do you take me for?"

"Very, very bad for the enamel. Tsk tsk. Now where does it hurt?"

Father Gabriel told him. The doctor dipped a stick into a pinkish gel in a beaker and rubbed the stick against Father Gabriel's gums.

"It's gone," said Father Gabriel. "The pain is gone."

"It's only a topical," said the doctor.

"The pain is gone. One touch and you have taken it away. How can I ever thank you? Oh, I feel like I'm alive again!"

"It will wear off shortly. Sit down, please."

"You have taken the pain away." Father Gabriel clambered out of the chair and pulled off the bib they had fastened around his neck. "I feel like myself again."

"I have not completed the exam," said the doctor.

"I misjudged you," said Father Gabriel. "I misjudged your people. You have given me my life back."

"I will not be responsible for this."

"You've given my life back and I will never forget it."

"I don't think he was finished," said Pete, when they were in the parking lot.

"Oh, look," said Father Gabriel. "Look how beautiful everything is. I don't want to go back yet. I want to go to the ocean. It's years since I've seen the ocean. The great Pacific! You'll take me, won't you?"

17

On the way, Father Gabriel laughed and pointed at everything moving past the windows of the Jeep, repeating, "Look–oh, look!"

Pete had to keep his eyes on the traffic. "Father," he said. "There are many things I have to tell you."

"I know, I know. But not now. Not yet. For the moment I am happy. Look at that–a big fat cigar floating in the sky! There really are miracles in the world." Pete glanced up. It was true. There was a big cigar in the sky. A bright banner flapped in the clear air behind it.

Father Gabriel went on chattering happily the whole way, delighted with all he saw. The sight of the ocean silenced him, but it did not stop his joy. Pete could see it still in his face. They stood together on the shore, the sea stretching before them, blue and measureless. On both sides the beach gave way to the slopes of faraway hills peaked with low clouds. Before them, the distance–a great blue shimmer–had no end. The sky widened above them as if it were spreading its arms to hold all that was below. The ocean's sound was everywhere, even though it was only a whisper, a gentle shushing that rose and fell but never stopped. In its tender way, it said to be quiet, and look, and that is what they did.

"Look–there's a Ferris wheel!" said Father Gabriel after a long while. "Let's go." He jumped up from where he had been sitting on the beach and hurried off, brushing sand from the seat of his robe. Pete followed.

The Ferris wheel was at the end of a pier. They edged their way through crowds that stood watching acrobats and street performers or milled around hot dog stands and soda fountains. A fat man chomping on a cigar helped them into their car. "We don't get many of your types around here," he said. "But bless your heart."

Father Gabriel pointed at his cigar. "We just saw one of those floating in the sky," he beamed.

They were lifted up. Little by little, they rose. Even as they did, the sky did not seem to come any closer, but the ocean stretched farther away. The horizon drew back and vanished. Father Gabriel caught his breath. “It’s the top of the world,” he murmured.

“We’re very, very high,” Pete agreed.

“It’s the top of the world,” Father Gabriel repeated crossly.

“Father, what are we going to do?”

Father Gabriel sighed. “I’m going to go back and face the music and you are going to go off and live your life. It is time. Long past time, I would say.”

Pete looked down. “Where will I go?”

“Home.”

“I haven’t got a home.”

“You’ll make one.”

“I don’t know how.”

“Then you’ll do without. Look at all

those people down there. They're doing without. Didn't you see their clothes spread around them on the ground where they slept? You haven't had a home for a long time. We can't live in the world and we can't live anywhere else. Do you want to go on living as a ghost?"

"No."

"Then what do you want?"

"I want not to want."

An airplane crossed the sky above them. It went higher and higher, then turned on its wing, circling back. Its movement was slow. Its sound was swallowed by the throb of the sea.

"Brother Dominic, you know," said Father Gabriel, "is the only one who ever comes to confession these days. Isn't it odd? I sit hunched in that booth twiddling my thumbs, and he is the only one. And he is quite the little blabbermouth, I must say."

Pete met his eyes. "Then you know."

"If your question is how long can one live without revelation, the answer is forever. 'He fashioned all things that they might have *being*.' If you have to remember any of it, remember that. And now there is one last thing I have to tell you."

Father Gabriel told him what it was. It changed everything. Pete knew what he would have to do. His heart opened. It was as if he had the ocean inside him. Yet he was also filled with rage. He wept, and Father Gabriel took him in his arms.

"You should have told me before," said Pete. "All this time I've lost."

"I'm terribly sorry, my boy. I haven't been in my right mind for years. Please forgive me, Pete."

"Why didn't you tell me before?"

"I'm telling you now," said Father Gabriel. "We have to start somewhere."

On the way back to the Jeep, they weaved through crowds along the boardwalk. Sellers spread their wares out everywhere. There were blankets across the ground covered with polished shells and charms for sale, bins and easels filled with colorful drawings, musicians playing their many different instruments in a babble of music that almost drowned out the sound of the sea. A little girl with a ponytail was sitting at a plain folding table. On the tabletop were a little red plastic tube and a square of cardboard. The girl sat with her hands folded on the table in front of her.

"What is it that you are selling, young lady?" asked Father Gabriel.

"Oops. I forgot," said the girl. She picked up a small pink purse from the ground beside her and set it on the table. She unsnapped its bright gold clasp. The only thing inside was a roll of tape. The girl leaned forward and taped the piece of cardboard to the edge of the table so that it hung down in front. In red magic marker, it said, GLIMPSES OF INFINITY—*one dollar*.

"You are selling glimpses of infinity?"

"That's right. Would you like one?"

"Very much so."

"One dollar, please."

Father Gabriel placed the bill into the empty purse. The girl handed him the red tube. It had little plastic see-through circles at each end. They were smudged with fingerprints. Father Gabriel peered into one end of the tube.

"That's the wrong side," said the girl.

Father Gabriel turned the tube around.

"You're still doing it wrong. You've got to hold it up."

He did. He looked into it for a long time, his face slowly changing. "Oh my," he said. "Oh my. I never dreamed." He handed the tube to Pete. All Pete saw were two straight lines, very close to each other. But as he watched, they grew even closer, without seeming to move at all, until bit by bit there was only a single line. Then, very slowly, the line disappeared, and all Pete was looking at was an empty circle in a wash of yellow light.

"Have you ever seen anything like it?" asked Father Gabriel, taking back the tube.

"No," said Pete. "I never have."

Father Gabriel set the tube carefully on the table. "Thank you very, very much, young lady."

"That's another dollar," said the girl, pointing at Pete. "He looked too."

18

When they got back, the superiors were waiting for them. “Where have you been?” demanded the Bishop. “We’ve been waiting here for hours.”

“I didn’t know Your Eminences were coming,” said Father Gabriel, spreading his arms in welcome. “Your Eminences did not tell me when to expect Your Eminences.”

The Abbot stepped forward. “Well?” he rasped.

“I was away doing the work assigned to me by Your Eminences. Then I went to the dentist. That took some time. Then, if the truth be told, we went to the beach. Each life needs a little ease. All work and no play, you know. And finally we had a glimpse of infinity. It was quite a day."

"What nonsense is this? Do you mean to be impertinent?"

The Abbot was a tall man, bald except for curly tufts of gray hair bubbling over both ears. The Bishop was short and grossly obese, which lent a special air to his sermons against gluttony.

"The thought never crossed my mind, Your Eminence," answered Father Gabriel.

"Perhaps you need to be reminded of the high office of the church," said the Bishop. "The church, that turned the cannibals to faith. The church, that brought light to every dark corner of the earth."

"I assure Your Eminences, I have never lost sight of those accomplishments," said Father Gabriel.

"One would never know it from how you conduct yourself," said the Abbot. "The time you kept us waiting we have put to good use. We have looked the place over from top to bottom. We left no stone unturned. We have never seen such sloth."

"It's not bad enough to bring in the police," said the Bishop. "No, that embarrassment to the church is not enough for you. An abbey is like a garden. You have not tended yours well. The weeds are in every crevice."

"Could Your Eminences be more specific?"

"It is an aura," said the Abbot. "And it is everywhere, like a rank smell. An aura of something terribly wrong. Something … unseemly."

"We feel it in our bones," said the Bishop. "There is nothing godly here. And we have seen the chaos with our own two eyes."

Pete thought Father Gabriel might be considering correcting him, since the total number of eyes was actually four. Instead, after a pause, Father Gabriel said, "Surely Your Eminences will agree that it is out of chaos that order comes."

"We are not here to discuss theology," snapped the Abbot. "We find grave fault in you. Measures will need to be taken, Father Gabriel. Definite measures."

It was then that a man came running into the foyer where they stood. He was whooping and howling. He twirled about the room, spinning on his feet. He waved his arms and cried out in broken words. His shouts formed a language of their own. He leaped into the air over and over, and flung himself against the walls. Finally, he scurried in a circle, tripped over the loose board, and fell flat on his face, out cold.

Everyone stood silent for a long moment. The Bishop and the Abbot looked stunned.

At last the Bishop spoke in a low, quaking voice. “Who is this man?”

Before an answer came, the Abbot cried, “This man is touched with the spirit of the Almighty Holy Ghost. Did you see him take to the air? Did you hear his gift of tongues? He is in the image of Saint Joseph, whose holy fits began three hundred and sixty years ago this very day—on the glorious Feast of our blessed Saint Francis!"

"Father Gabriel, perhaps we have been too hasty," said the Bishop. "Revive this man, that he might tell us of his inspiration."

Just then the door flew open. Brother Louis stood in the doorway. He glanced at Brother Walter lying on the floor. Then he said, "The barn's on fire. But I caught the intruder. I've got him tied to a tree."

19

The straw fed the flames, and the wood was very dry. The door had fallen shut and, as was its way, it was jammed and would not open. Pete threw himself against it over and over. "Neb, Neb's in there," he screamed. "Please, please, somebody–help her, save her." Brother Louis ran to the tool shed and came back with a hatchet. He began to chop furiously at the door, but flames crept out from under it, then shot up, and soon they had worked their way from the ground and flared in all directions as they consumed the wood and raced toward the roof, where they thrashed at the darkness above. It was no use. Father Gabriel pulled Pete away from the fire and held him there. Brother Louis dropped the hatchet to the ground and fell to his knees with a terrible moan. The walls of the barn fell in. Plumes of smoke shot into the sky.

The police arrived first. Officer Stingo and Officer Lund reported to Father Gabriel. "There's an animal trapped in the barn," Father Gabriel told them.

"Firemen are on the way," said Office Stingo. "But it don't look good, sir."

"Could somebody please tend to Brother Walter?" Father Gabriel asked. "He's just inside. He tripped on a loose board."

"I warned you about that, sir," Officer Lund said sternly.

They turned to the bearded man tied to a tree by his neck. The butt of a burnt-out cigarette was clenched between his teeth. He told them he had no name. "No worries," said Officer Stingo with the pride of one who had finally got his man. He grabbed the stranger's wrist and held up his hand. "He has fingerprints. Those are even better."

By the time the fire trucks got there, the barn was nothing but a heap of blazing wood. A photo appeared in the next day's papers. It had been taken from a distance. No one knew by whom. It showed many men running this way and that, surrounding the fire, hoisting thick hoses that coiled about the yard like serpents. It showed the Bishop and the Abbot huddled together in a corner of the picture, with expressions of fear and confusion. It showed a wild-haired, snickering man tied by his neck to a tree, which raised concerns about proper procedure among citizens who wrote letters to the editor. It showed a small group of monks standing in a circle with kindly, troubled looks on their faces and, in the middle of the circle, kneeling among them, a young man whose whole body was wracked with such grief that, had it been seen more closely, it might have been unbearable to witness. No casualties were reported.

The photo showed a scene of great turmoil. If it was true that order came from chaos, then all should have been well by the morning. But it was a very long night.

20

Pete left the next day just before dusk. He had brought little with him and took little away. He had left his Bible on the table in his cell, which was otherwise empty now.

What Father Gabriel had told him was that his mother had been there, soon after Pete arrived. She had not come to see Pete, but to see Father Gabriel. She wanted him to tell her that he would take good care of Pete. He assured her that he would. Then she told Father Gabriel about Michael. She told him she had letters from Michael to Pete. She did not know what to do with them, but she had saved them. She kept them hidden from Pete's father. She could not condone them or what they meant, she said, and she was sure Father Gabriel would agree. Even so, Father Gabriel told her, Pete should have them. He suggested that she send them along, but they never came.

Pete's plan was to walk down to the village and sleep that night in the park. The next morning he would get a bus. Father Gabriel had given him money for the ticket. If his mother still had the letters, he would read them. He could scarcely imagine what they might say. But there were several. That meant something. He had not given up.

Was it possible that Pete could find him? Should he try? He would have to decide. He could not believe that Michael would still be waiting. He hoped not. He hoped he had lived. So many years had gone by.

That afternoon he had heard Father Gabriel speak one last time. He spoke of Christ's wounds, his torn hands, his crown of thorns. "Do you know what love is?" he asked gently. "It is the suffering of those nails. See Christ on the cross. *See* him. Learn from that how to love." He ended as he always would now, by putting in a good word for the Hindus. The men listened closely and lifted their heads and said, "Amen."

"That was lovely," Pete said afterward.

"It's just words, of course," said Father Gabriel. "But we'll see. We'll see."

"Brother Louis wasn't there."

"He's taking it hard about the mule."

"Neb was a donkey," said Pete. "I think Brother Louis may be a true believer."

"I think so too," said Father Gabriel. "It's a pity, isn't it?"

Soon Pete would sleep under the stars, as he and Michael had imagined they might. He stopped near a patch of dandelions by the path. Neb loved dandelions. Pete picked one. He felt the tears coming again, but he resisted. He would always mourn her, but he had had enough of sadness for now. He sucked the sap from the dandelion's stalk. It tasted sweet.

He put the flower in his pocket and started down the road.

Neb watched him go. She was sitting in a ditch at the edge of the woods with her legs folded under her. The ditch was shallow enough that she could see over a ridge up the hill if she lifted her head a little. Her heart leaped up when she saw him, as it always had. But she did not bray. If he knew she was there, she thought he might stay. She let him go.

She had only cried twice before. It felt strange. For a long time she had lived with an old woman. She had loved the old woman and thought she was kind. But the woman gave Neb's child away. Still, Neb had not cried then. It was only later, when she realized her child would not be coming back. That was when she cried, and it was when she first knew that she could tell the future.

It came in handy. It was how she had known to kick loose the planks at the back of the barn, so she could still get out if the door stuck. She had known this would happen. It was the man who beat her who had let her out of her stall. That she had not predicted. It was after he nabbed the scoundrel who'd set the place on fire that he had set her free. If it hadn't been for that, she would have been a goner. She thought maybe she should forgive him for everything else he had done. But no. On second thought, she wouldn't. After all, he hadn't kept the door from shutting.

A little black cat had come wandering by that afternoon. It saw Neb sitting in the ditch and came up to her and nipped at her sides. Neb guessed that it thought it might get some milk. When it found it couldn't, it nestled beside her. Now Neb felt it pressed against her, purring. The poor little thing had patchy fur and a tattered ear. Something had chewed its ear off. It was so small. Neb had no idea how they survived, these little things. She figured she would take care of the cat for a while.

She hadn't slept all night. She was tired, but she was thinking too much. She thought again of the old woman. The second time she cried it had been for her. It was very strange, because Neb thought her heart had turned against the old woman after she had given away her child. But it was something Neb heard her say long after that, when Neb herself was given away.

"Be good with her," the old woman said to the people who took her, as Neb was being led off. "She was all I ever had."

What else could you do, Neb thought, but cry.

In the distance, up the hill, Pete stooped to pick a dandelion. Seeing this reminded Neb that she was hungry. But she did not think she should stir just yet, because it might wake up the cat.

She watched Pete going down the road until he disappeared. She knew she would not see him again. He had been a good friend. She hoped everything would work out for him. She knew it would. She knew it, not just because she could tell the future, but because she had faith. She had faith in him.

It was not long after dark that she finally fell asleep.